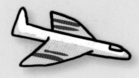
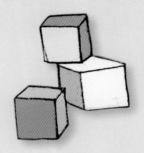

# This igloo book belongs to:

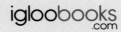

*Published in 2012*
*by Igloo Books Ltd*
*Cottage Farm*
*Sywell*
*NN6 0BJ*
*www.igloobooks.com*

*Copyright© 2012 Igloo Books Ltd*

*SHE001 0812*
*2 4 6 8 10 9 7 5 3 1*
*ISBN 978-0-85780-569-0*

*Printed and manufactured in China*
*Illustrated by Richard Watson*

# My First Stories for Boys

igloobooks
.com

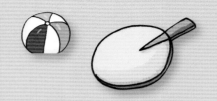
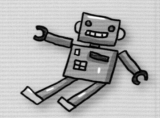

# Contents

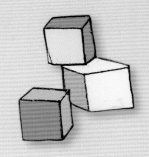

# The Great Explorer

"I'm going to be an explorer," said Jack, as he put on his
best explorer's hat. "That sounds exciting," said Mum.
"Watch out for creepy crawlies, scary spiders and things that buzz."

"Silly Mum," said Jack. "Explorers aren't afraid of creepy crawlies."
He grabbed his backpack, net and magnifying glass
and dashed out the door to start exploring.

At the pond, Jack looked through his giant magnifying glass. "There's something under the water," he whispered. SPLASH! A big, green frog jumped up and landed right next to him.

"CRROOAK!" went the big, fat frog. It made Jack jump.

He ran across the grass, but the frog hopped along behind him.

"I'll hide by the fence so he can't get me," thought Jack.

Jack watched from the fence as the frog hopped away.
Suddenly, there was a loud buzzing, zuzzing sound. It was a giant
bumble bee, flying straight towards him.

The bee came closer and closer. "Help!" cried Jack.
He stumbled back and fell right into a big spider's web.
"Yuck!" he cried. "I'm covered in sticky stuff."

An enormous spider sat on top of Jack's hat. "I've had enough of creepy crawlies," he thought. Just then, his tummy began to rumble. "I'm hungry and I want to go home."

Jack ran inside where Mum gave him a big hug and made him some lovely sandwiches. "How was your day exploring?" she asked. "Being an explorer was great," said Jack, "but coming home is even better."

# When I Met the Moon

Every night, Alex looked out of his bedroom window.
"I wish I could fly to the moon in a bright red rocket," he said.
Then, one night, his wish came true.

"All aboard the red rocket," said a voice. Alex jumped out of bed and into the rocket. It flew with a WHOOSH up towards the stars and planets.

15

Bump, thump, went the rocket as it landed on the moon.
Alex climbed out and met some friendly, little moonlings.
"Welcome to the moon," they said. "Come and play with us."

16

Alex and the moonlings jumped over moon craters and
threw moon rocks in a game of space-ball. They played hide-and-seek,
giggling as they peeked out from behind the rocket.

It was very tiring having fun on the moon. "I'd better go home now," said Alex, yawning. "Have some moon cheese to take with you," said the moonlings. "Goodbye. Come back soon."

Back in his room, Alex snuggled into his warm, cozy bed and thought of the moonlings and all the fun things they had done. "I must go to the moon again," he said, as he fell into a lovely, dreamy sleep.

# My Friends and Me

My name is Leo and I've got the best friends ever.
I love it when they visit me and we all play together.
Bobby likes to draw a lot and Joey plays the clown,
He's always doing hand stands, walking upside down.

Sam likes to look for creepy things crawling on the ground.
When Danny sees a spider, he squeals and runs around.
There's just so much for us to do, so many games to play,
We giggle and we chase around, having fun all day.

The game that we all like the best is football in the park.
We run and jump and kick the ball until the sky goes dark.
Sam and Joey chase me when I kick the ball away.
I shoot it right into the net and Danny shouts, "Hurray."

When playtime's over we feel tired and ready for our beds.
We stretch and yawn and snuggle down, we're such sleepyheads.
That is why my friends and I have so much fun together.
They'll always come to play with me, we'll be best friends forever.

# Hide and Seek

It was a lovely, sunny day on the farm. "Let's play hide and seek." said Polly. "I'm brilliant at hide and seek," said Polly's brother, James. "You'll never find me."

Polly covered her eyes and slowly counted from
one to ten. "The hen house is the perfect place to hide," thought James,
as he ran across the farmyard.

"CLUCK, CLUCK, SQUAWK!" went the chickens, flapping their wings. "Shh! Polly will hear you," said James, as he tried to squeeze through the door. "You hens are too noisy. I'll hide in the stables instead."

James ran into the stables and hid in the hay. Just then, there was a loud clip-clopping noise. "NEIGH!" went Neddy the horse. "He's so big," thought James. "I'd better hide outside instead."

James dashed into the field and hid behind the fence.
Suddenly, a huge, "MOO!" scared him. It was Cassie the cow,
swishing her tail. "Oh, no," said James, running away.

"I'm coming, ready or not!" yelled Polly. James quickly looked around for a place to hide. He dived into the pigsty and hid among the pigs. "She'll never find me in here," he said.

Suddenly, he noticed a terrible smell. "Yuck! This pig pen pongs!"
thought James, holding his nose. "I can't stand it!" He ran as fast as
he could into the field and bumped straight into Polly.

"I found you!" cried Polly. "Now it's my turn to hide."
"I think we should play a different game," said James, laughing.
"Hiding on a farm really stinks!"

# I Don't Like Custard!

There were lots of things that Ben didn't like. He didn't like vegetables for dinner. "Yuck!" he said, flicking a brussels sprout away. "I don't like these, they taste horrible."

Ben didn't like his dessert either. It slipped and slopped off his spoon like a slimy bogey. "I can't eat that," he moaned. "I don't like runny custard."

Ben didn't like it when it rained. "I don't like rainy days," he said, frowning at the sploshy raindrops outside. "I can't go outside and play."
"Why don't you do a jigsaw puzzle instead?" said Dad.

Ben didn't like jigsaw puzzles either. He tried really hard, but there were pieces missing. "I don't like missing jigsaw pieces," grumbled Ben.

When the rain stopped, Ben put on a coat and went outside, running straight into a puddle. The water splashed over the top of his boots and soaked his socks. "I don't like soggy socks!" he moaned.

Just then, Ben's friends arrived. "Come and play football," they said. The sun came out and they played all afternoon. "Playing is loads of fun," said Ben.  At long last he had found something he liked!

# Just Like Dad

Tom loved his Dad. He wanted to be just like him. "I'll go and help in the garden," said Tom. "I'll wear my best boots and water the flowers, just like Dad."

Tom turned on the hosepipe and the water went SWOOSH!
It wiggled and jiggled everywhere. Tom was soaked.
"Oh, no," he said. "I'm all wet."

Tom's boots went squelch, squelch, as he walked inside.
He put on Dad's big, blue jumper and comfy slippers, but when he looked
in the mirror, he felt silly. Dad's clothes were far too big.

Tom gave up and slumped into Dad's favorite chair. He turned on the TV and read a comic. Then, Mom came into the room and laughed. "You look just like your Dad," she said. Tom smiled happily.

# Rory's Bedtime Rhyme

I've been playing all day and now there's no doubt,
That I'm feeling quite sleepy and all tired out.
Mom sees that I'm mucky, all covered in grime,
She says, "Have a bath and then it's bedtime."

She puts lots of bubbles in my lovely bath,
They tickle my toes and make me want to laugh.
I play with my duck while Mom washes my hair,
Then I get dry and decide what to wear.

When I brush my teeth, I dream of the stars,
I imagine I'm zooming past Venus and Mars.
In my rocket pajamas, I can be a space man,
I'll whizz round the planets, as fast as I can.

I look out the window and wave at the moon,
I know in my dreams, I'll be going there soon.
I pick up my teddy and climb into bed,
Pull up the covers and lay down my head.

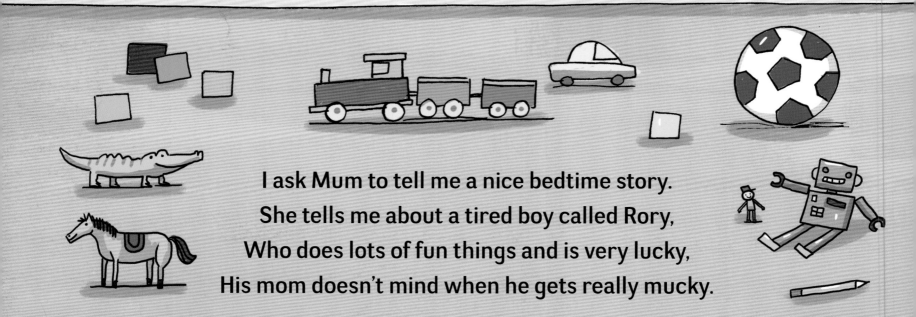

I ask Mum to tell me a nice bedtime story.
She tells me about a tired boy called Rory,
Who does lots of fun things and is very lucky,
His mom doesn't mind when he gets really mucky.

Now I'm snuggly and warm, Mom whispers goodnight,
She gives me a kiss and turns off my light.
Then it's straight off to sleep to dream lovely dreams,
Until I wake up with the morning sunbeams.

# Josh Makes a Splash

Josh didn't like swimming. He was afraid of the water.
When his dad took him to the pool, he hid under his towel.

Josh's brother and sister loved swimming. "Wheee!" SPLOSH, they went, as they jumped in. "I wish I could swim like them," thought Josh.

"Maybe I'll just try paddling in the shallow end," thought Josh.
SPLISH, SPLASH, SPLOSH went the other swimmers, as they raced by.
"I'll never be able to swim like that," he said.

"Don't worry," said Dad. "You just need to kick your legs and move your arms." Josh tried really hard, but water went up his nose and in his ears. "I don't like it," he said.

All Josh could do was watch his brother and sister
having a lovely time in the pool while he clung to the side.
"I'm just no good at swimming," he sobbed.

"I've got an idea," said Dad, smiling. Josh watched as his dad
went off to talk to the lifeguard. When Dad came back, he was holding a
red rubber ring. "What's that?" asked Josh.

Dad showed Josh how to use the special ring.
"It will help you float," he said. Before long, Josh was happily splashing around in the water with his brother and sister.

Josh splished and splashed with everyone in the pool. They laughed and giggled and all joined in. "I'm not scared of the water anymore," said Josh. "From now on, I know that swimming is going to be loads of fun!"

# Teddy Gets Wet

Eddie felt sad. "I've lost my teddy!" he cried.
"He isn't on my bed, or in the toy box."
"Maybe he's behind the sofa?" said Dad.

56

Eddie searched behind the sofa and under the cushions,
but Teddy wasn't there. Suddenly, he heard a very strange sound.
Splosh, whirr, thump! Splosh, whirr, thump!

Eddie followed the strange noise all the way to the washing machine.

"Oh, no!" he gasped. "Teddy's trapped in the washer!"

"He's getting dizzy spinning round with all those bubbles."

"Don't worry," said Mum. "Teddy's just having a special wash."
She took Teddy out of the washer and hung him on the line where
he drip, drip, dripped. Eddie watched his bear dry all day.

By bedtime, Eddie's teddy was all dry. Eddie climbed into bed and snuggled his fluffy, clean bear. "Mmm, you smell lovely," said Eddie. When Mom came to read Eddie a story, he smiled at her.

"Thank you for giving Teddy a sploshy wash," said Eddie.
"Now he's the softest, fluffiest bear ever."
"Goodnight, Teddy," said Eddie.

# My Shadow and Me

One day, in my back garden, something followed me.
It crept across the grass, along the wall and up the tree.

"Who are you?" I asked, but I don't think that it heard.
It just followed me around and never said a word.

The shape slid down my slide and swung on my blue swing.
I ran to tell my mom, but she couldn't see a thing.

I pointed at the grass, as the strange shape moved about.
"That's your shadow," said Mom. "It appears when the sun comes out."

Now, I make my shadow move. I make it jump and bend.
It's not scary anymore. It's my very special friend.

# My Brilliant Mom

When Charlie lost his teddy bear, he looked all through his toys and pulled things out of his closet, but he couldn't find Teddy anywhere.

Luckily, Mom was there to help. "Here's Teddy," she said, lifting up a pile of clothes. "Thanks, Mom," said Charlie, hugging his bear. "You're brilliant!"

Charlie loved going to the park, but sometimes he fell
over and scraped his knee. "OUCH!" he cried, but Mom was always
there to make Charlie feel all better.

Once, when Charlie had no one to play with, Mom burst
into the room with a pirate's hat and a toy sword. "It's pirate Mom,"
she said. "Let's sail the seven seas!"

When Charlie was hungry, his tummy made lots of noise.
"What a growly, grumbly tummy!" said Mom. "You need some yummy
sandwiches." She always knew just what to do to make
Charlie's rumbly tummy go away.

On rainy days, Charlie got muddy jumping in puddles. Mom ran
a lovely, warm bath and filled it to the top with bubbles that popped
when Charlie splashed. "Thank you, Mom," said Charlie.

Charlie and Mom loved to read together. They always read Charlie's favorite story about dragons. "ROAR!" went Mom, as she did all the actions with Charlie's dragon puppet.

Mom did lots of lovely things for Charlie.
"I love you, Mom," whispered Charlie, cuddling up close. "I think you're brilliant. You're the best mom ever."

# My Little Sister

George wasn't sure he liked his little sister, Emmy. She pushed over the tower he had made with his building blocks. "I spent all morning building that," he said, but Emmy just giggled.

When George tried to play with his yellow truck, Emmy climbed into the back. George huffed and puffed to push the truck, but it wouldn't budge. "Get out, Emmy," he grumbled. "You're too heavy."

At lunch time, George was just about to eat a
yummy sandwich when Emmy spilled her milk all over it.
"Oh, no," he moaned. "My sandwich is all soggy."

That afternoon, George spent ages painting a picture of
a rainbow. Then, Emmy crawled right over it. George felt very cross.
"She's ruined my picture!" he cried.

"Never mind," said Mom, giving George a lovely cuddle. "Perhaps you could help me give Emmy a bath. She's all covered in paint."

78

In the bath, Emmy splished and splashed, making
George giggle. They had a wonderful time together.
"Maybe little sisters aren't so bad after all," he said, smiling.

# Pirate Fun

"I want to be a pirate," said Robby, one sunny day.
"I'll put on my best captain's hat and shout, 'Anchors away!'

I'll bring my shipmates, Tim and Tom, and Bill my parrot, too,
I'll have such great adventures, exploring with my crew."

"We'll sail to desert islands, where big sharks swim around,
And bury all our treasure, so it's hidden underground.

We'll check the map and hoist the sail, then steer back out to sea.
One thing I am sure of, it's a pirate's life for me!"

# Messy Monsters

Billy had an imaginary friend. It was a big, blue monster!
Billy and his monster went everywhere together and whatever
the monster did, Billy did, too.

"I bet there's treasure buried in the back garden," said Billy's monster, one morning. So, Billy dug and dug, but he didn't find any treasure. "Stop that!" yelled Dad, running outside. "You're ruining my flowers."

Billy and the monster were covered from head-to-toe in dirt after
all that digging. "Let's make muddy handprints on the walls," said
Billy's monster. Mom wasn't very happy. "It was  my monster's idea," said Billy.

Later, Billy's monster said, "Let's make a den out of all the pillows in the house." It was great fun, but the feathers went everywhere. Billy blamed that on the monster, too. "What a naughty monster!" said Mom.

At dinner time, Billy didn't eat any vegetables. "Monsters don't eat peas and carrots, Mom," he said. "They eat cookies and cakes." "What a fussy monster," said Mom.

When it was bath time, Billy and the monster had a water fight.
They splashed water and bubbles everywhere, slipping and slopping and
having a great time. "What a messy monster," said Dad.

When it was time for bed, Billy and his monster snuggled
under the covers. Mom walked into the room looking very suprised.
"It's so tidy in here," she said. "There are no muddy handprints,
or feathers, or splashes."

"My monster helped me to tidy up after our very messy day," said Billy, yawning. "What a good monster," said Mom, smiling. "Goodnight Billy, goodnight Monster."

# Big and Small

Harry loved his older brother, Joey. He wanted to be just like him. When Joey rode his shiny, blue bike, Harry wanted to ride it, too. "You're too small, Harry," said Joey.

When Joey climbed a big tree, Harry wanted to climb it too, but he couldn't even reach the lowest branch. "You're just too little to climb up here," said Joey.

Joey liked to play football with his friends. "I want to kick the ball, too," said Harry. "This game is just for big kids," said Joey.

"It's not fair," thought Harry. "I'm too little to do anything." Suddenly, the ball whooshed past his head and through a small hole in the fence. "Oh, no!" said Joey. "We'll never get our ball back now."

"I'll get it!" shouted Harry, crawling through the hole and grabbing the ball. "Well done, Harry," said Joey, cheering. "It's lucky you were here, we couldn't have done it without you."